For the staff of Saint Brigid of Kildare Preschool,
for whom I am truly thankful.

Published in association with
Bear With Us Productions

ISBN 979-8-9883636-0-6

Brand by Richie Evans
Design by Emma Evans
Illustrated by Felipe Calv
www.justbearwithus.com

THANKFUL FUR YOU!

Written by
Hillary Harper

Illustrated by
Felipe Calv

On a November afternoon,
Cannoli and his owner, Cami,
were out for their daily walk.
The air was brisk, and the wind
blew leaves along the street.

The weather was just right
for playing in his yard and
taking a walk.

BEWARE
OF DOG!

It also meant his favorite holiday, Thanksgiving, would be soon.

Cannoli loved Thanksgiving. Cami would sneak him extra treats during dinner – turkey, stuffing, and mashed potatoes!

Family and friends filled the house with food and delicious smells. Drifting off to sleep that night, Cannoli dreamed of all the **wonders** Thanksgiving would bring.

The next morning on their walk, Cami and Cannoli passed by the shops in town. All the windows were filled with holiday decorations.

Cami said, "Christmas keeps coming earlier and earlier each year. It seems like Thanksgiving doesn't exist anymore."

Oh no! Cannoli thought. **Is Thanksgiving canceled?**

The next day, they headed to the dog park. Cannoli's friends, Mack and Mr. Oinks, were waiting for him. They looked worried.

"Something is wrong," whimpered Mr. Oinks. "My owner said, who needs Thanksgiving when Christmas is on its way. I think she's going to cancel Thanksgiving!"

"My owner said the same thing!" barked Mack. "She's already hung Christmas lights in our yard!"

Cannoli could not believe what his friends were saying. **"Why would they cancel our favorite holiday?"** he asked.

"Well... I **chewed** up my owner's slippers yesterday." ruffed Mr. Oinks.

"I **barked** at the little girl who lives next door. She kept running through my yard," said Mack.

"I **rolled** in a mud puddle,

Cami said I looked like a zebra
instead of a dog," added Cannoli.

The dogs thought they could try a little harder to show their owners how **thankful** they were.

"Thanksgiving is not just about food," Cannoli said. "It is a time to show people how much you **love** and **appreciate** them."

"We have to show our owners how thankful we are for them!" barked Mr. Oinks.

"Yes, then they will remember how much they love us," ruffed Mack.

"And they won't cancel Thanksgiving!" yelped Cannoli.

Cannoli headed home from the dog park,
thinking of ways he could show Cami how
thankful he was.

He would be on his best behavior,
and Thanksgiving would be saved!

The next day, Cannoli played in his yard and did not get dirty. It was really hard to stay clean, but he knew he could do it!

When Cami let him in the house,
he was still white and fluffy.

"You are my **best boy**, Cannoli.
Thank you for not getting mucky!"
said Cami.

While they were on their walk, Cannoli usually pulled
on the leash so he could sniff the mailbox, but not today.
He walked nicely on his leash.

"What a good boy!" Cami beamed at him.

For the next few days, he was on his best behavior. No barking at the neighbors. No chasing birds. He even stopped eating out of the trash can!

It was exhausting!

He had to show Cami how thankful he was for her.

"**Are you OK, Cannoli?**"
Cami asked.

"You haven't gotten dirty, or sniffed the mailboxes, or eaten from the trash can. I'm worried about you. I know those things drive me crazy, but I love you just the way you are!"

Cannoli thought about this. She loves me just the way I am! Cami is thankful for me! Maybe Thanksgiving isn't canceled after all.

Finally, it was the fourth Thursday in November.

Cannoli paced back and forth in the living room.

He could smell

something delicious cooking. He ran into the kitchen.

Cami was making **Thanksgiving food!**
His favorite holiday was saved!

Soon after, the doorbell rang.
It was Mack, Mr. Oinks,
and their owners.
They had come for
Thanksgiving dinner.

"I really tried to be a good boy," said Mr. Oinks.

"Me too!" ruffed Mack.

"They are **thankful for us** just the way we are," barked Cannoli.

After eating their special feast, Cannoli
and Cami curled up on the couch with full bellies.

"I love you, Cannoli.
You are my best boy," gushed Cami.
Cannoli gave her a big kiss
and knew that he had
lots to be **thankful** for.

Made in United States
North Haven, CT
02 November 2023